My friend,
HAPPY

KT-409-880

AUTUMN PUBLISHING

I have a friend called Happy.

She **brightens** any day.

Whenever I feel worried,
she always comes to stay.

When Happy first appeared, I was feeling really sad.
She landed on my shoulder and she said, "It's not so bad!"

With Happy as my friend, I won't be scared at all.
She **chases** all my fears away when I am feeling small.

Now if I learn something new and things keep going wrong,

Happy's there to show me I could do it all along.

I love to play with my best friends out in the **shining** sun.

We **race** outside together, then we skip, leap, splash and run!

But when everyone is busy, and I am on my own,
Happy thinks of games to play. I'm not really alone!

At dance class, if I wobble and fall, **BUMP**, down on the ground,
Happy **sprinkles** magic dust and **swirls** it all around.

The sparkling dust **twinkles** and it has a special shine.
It helps me try the steps again and soon I feel just fine.

If I can't get to sleep at night,
and worries fill my head,
I close my eyes and I imagine
fairylands instead.

Happy swoops beside me in amazing, **magic** dreams,
and shows me that the dark is not as scary as it seems.

When I look out at my classmates, and think, "I can't run that fast!"
Happy makes sure I feel **proud** if sometimes I come last.

She tells me just how **thoughtful**, **kind** and **clever** I can be,
so instead of thinking I'm no good, I'm glad just to be me!

If I think there might be monsters,
just behind the bedroom door,
Happy helps me **peek**, and then
I'm not scared any more.

Or if there's a noisy storm,
with lightning **big** and **bright**,
she sits with me by the window
and soon everything's alright.

I'm sure I can do anything, with Happy by my side.
She makes me feel much **bolder**, so I never have to hide.

We can have adventures, or even sail the seven seas,
dance in **shining** spotlights or fly **high** up on the breeze.

If someone feels upset
and they begin to cry,
Happy will appear and
then **soar** into the sky.

"Close your eyes," I say, "and make a wish, just like a spell."

Then in a **flash** she's back, and Happy brings a friend as well!

No one else can see them, but we know they're always there
to spread a little **magic** and paint **rainbows** everywhere.

So the next time you feel worried, you'll know just what to do.
Close your eyes and make a **wish**...

... you'll find your Happy, too!

LIBRARIES NI
WITHDRAWN FROM STOCK

This book belongs to:

....

AUTUMN
PUBLISHING

Published in 2021
First published in the UK by Autumn Publishing
An imprint of Igloo Books Ltd
Cottage Farm, NN6 0BJ, UK
Owned by Bonnier Books
Sveavägen 56, Stockholm, Sweden
www.autumnpublishing.co.uk

Copyright © 2020 Autumn Publishing

All rights reserved. No part of this publication may be
reproduced or transmitted in any form or by any means,
electronic, or mechanical, including photocopying, recording,
or by any information storage and retrieval system,
without permission in writing from the publisher.

0521 001
2 4 6 8 10 9 7 5 3 1
ISBN 978-1-80022-294-6

Written by Hannah Campling
Illustrated by Siân Roberts

Designed by Hannah George
Edited by Hannah Campling

Printed and manufactured in China